Samuel French Acting Editi

MW00777099

Cardboard Piano

by Hansol Jung

SAMUELFRENCH.COM   SAMUELFRENCH.CO.UK

FOR PRODUCTION ENQUIRIES

UNITED STATES AND CANADA
Info@SamuelFrench.com
1-866-598-8449

UNITED KINGDOM AND EUROPE
Plays@SamuelFrench.co.uk
020-7255-4302

Each title is subject to availability from Samuel French, depending upon country of performance. Please be aware that *CARDBOARD PIANO* may not be licensed by Samuel French in your territory. Professional and amateur producers should contact the nearest Samuel French office or licensing partner to verify availability.

MUSIC USE NOTE

Licensees are solely responsible for obtaining formal written permission from copyright owners to use copyrighted music in the performance of this play and are strongly cautioned to do so. If no such permission is obtained by the licensee, then the licensee must use only original music that the licensee owns and controls. Licensees are solely responsible and liable for all music clearances and shall indemnify the copyright owners of the play(s) and their licensing agent, Samuel French, against any costs, expenses, losses and liabilities arising from the use of music by licensees. Please contact the appropriate music licensing authority in your territory for the rights to any incidental music.

IMPORTANT BILLING AND CREDIT REQUIREMENTS

If you have obtained performance rights to this title, please refer to your licensing agreement for important billing and credit requirements.

CARDBOARD PIANO was developed during a residency at the Eugene O'Neill Theater Center's National Playwrights Conference in 2015 (Preston Whiteway, Executive Director; Wendy C. Goldberg, Artistic Director).

CARDBOARD PIANO was first produced by the Humana Festival of New American Plays, Actors Theatre of Louisville at the Victor Jory Theatre on March 27, 2016. The performance was directed by Leigh Silverman, with sets by William Boles, costumes by Kaye Voyce, lighting by Keith Parham, sound by M.L. Dogg, original music and composition by Jason Webb, and dramaturgy by Hannah Rae Montgomery. The production stage manager was Jason Pacella. The cast was as follows:

CHRIS	Briana Pozner
ADIEL	Nike Kadri
PIKA	Jamar Williams
SOLDIER	Michael Luwoye
PAUL	Michael Luwoye
RUTH	Nike Kadri
FRANCIS	Jamar Williams

CHARACTERS

PART I

CHRIS (sixteen) – a child in love
ADIEL (sixteen) – a child in love
PIKA (thirteen) – a child soldier
SOLDIER – a soldier

PART II

CHRIS (thirty) – a visitor
PAUL (twenty-seven) – a pastor, Soldier from Part I
RUTH (twenty-nine) – a pastor's wife, Adiel from Part I
FRANCIS (twenty-two) – a local kid, Pika from Part I

SETTING

A township in Northern Uganda

TIME

Part I: New Year's Eve, 1999
Part II: A Wedding Anniversary, 2014

AUTHOR'S NOTES

–	a cut-off either by self or other
/	a point where another character might cut in
¶	a switch of thought
[ ]	things that aren't spoken in words
,	at end of a line marks an interruption of thought by another character, not necessarily a line cut-off

LUO TRANSLATIONS

jal – le	I surrender
apwoyo matek	Thank you very much
mzungu	(light-skinned) foreigner
Polo	Heaven
Jesu	Jesus
woko ki ii bal	out of sin
Aye tiyo tic pa lala	I decide to walk with God
ii kwo wa ii to	until I die

PART I

(Night.)

(A church – not one of stone and stained glass, more a small town hall dressed up to be a church. There's a hole in the roof of the church.)

(Two men, two women.)

(In separate spaces, they sing together, simple a capella that might blow up into something bigger and scarier.)

ALL.

JUST AS I AM, WITHOUT ONE PLEA[*],
BUT THAT THY BLOOD WAS SHED FOR ME,
AND THAT THOU BIDST ME COME TO THEE,
O LAMB OF GOD, I COME, I COME

JUST AS I AM, THOUGH TOSSED ABOUT
WITH MANY A CONFLICT, MANY A DOUBT,
FIGHTINGS AND FEARS WITHIN, WITHOUT,
O LAMB OF GOD, I COME, I COME

JUST AS I AM, THY LOVE UNKNOWN
HATH BROKEN EVERY BARRIER DOWN;
NOW, TO BE THINE, YEA, THINE ALONE,
O LAMB OF GOD, I COME, I COME

JUST AS I AM, OF THAT FREE LOVE
THE BREADTH, LENGTH DEPTH, AND HEIGHT TO PROVE,
HERE FOR A SEASON, THEN ABOVE,
O LAMB OF –

(Rain. Loud. Pours through the hole in the roof.)

---

[*] Hymn 313, Words by Charlotte Elliott, Music by William B. Bradbury.

> *(Pews, chair, cushions arranged to create a hollow in the middle of the church.)*

> *(**ADIEL**, age sixteen, is asleep in the middle of the hollow, strewn with wild flower petals.)*

> *(**CHRIS**, age sixteen, slips in, big suitcase in tow.)*

> *(She hides the suitcase somewhere in the shadows. She tiptoes around the chairs and benches to lean into **ADIEL**'s sleeping ear.)*

> *(Whispers.)*

CHRIS. The end of the world is near.

> *(**ADIEL** starts.)*

ADIEL. Hm?!

CHRIS. Hi.

ADIEL. Where am, what,

CHRIS. It's me, just me.

ADIEL. For heaven's sake Chris. You frightened me. What is the time. You are very late.

CHRIS. Had to wait till the folks fell asleep.

ADIEL. Your parents?

> *(**CHRIS** finds party blower.)*

CHRIS. Blowers!

ADIEL. Why are they still here?

CHRIS. Blue one's mine!

ADIEL. What about the party? What happened?

CHRIS. Nothing. They didn't wanna go, I guess.

ADIEL. So your parents are still in the house?

CHRIS. It's fine. They went to bed. Said they wanna be up in time to see the ball fall in New York.
Miss me?

ADIEL. I saw you just three hours ago.

CHRIS. We didn't know if the world was gonna end, three hours ago.

ADIEL. It did not.

(CHRIS blows on blower: yay!)

Shh!

CHRIS. Happy New Year.

ADIEL. Happy New Year. You'll wake them up.

(Blow.)

Chris it is not funny –

(Blow.)

Come now give it to me.

CHRIS. Make me.

(Blow.)

ADIEL. Haw this is a challenge now?

(ADIEL jumps CHRIS, misses.)

CHRIS. Prepare for battle!

(Battle trumpets blowblowblow.)

Upon my honor I shall never surrender!

(Bloooooooooooooooooooooooooo –)

(Blowing stops because ADIEL kisses her.)

I surrender.

(Kiss.)

How do you say I surrender in Luo?

ADIEL. *Jal – le.*

CHRIS. *Jal – le.*

ADIEL. I am very sexy when you speak my language.

CHRIS. I am sexy.

ADIEL. You too?

CHRIS. No, I am sexy, to you. Sexy is a thing I am, that makes You want to get into My pants.

ADIEL. Why are we turning this into English lesson?

CHRIS. I am very sexy when you speak my language wrong.

ADIEL. So both ways we are very sexy.

CHRIS. Okay.

(Hands in pants, hairs undone, shirts flung off, skirts riding up –)

(Thunder and lightning.)

CHRIS. Woah.

*(**CHRIS** bolts upright like a meerkat.)*

ADIEL. What is the matter?

CHRIS. Think he's mad at us?

ADIEL. Who?

CHRIS. I'd be mad if people came to my house at night, mess it up, have sex all over my cushions in front of a picture of me hanging naked on a tree –

*(**ADIEL** kisses **CHRIS**.)*

ADIEL. I think he is thrilled we included him.

CHRIS. We didn't.

ADIEL. Well I did and I think he is saying congratulations on your big day!

(Thunder.)

(Meerkat.)

He is happy for us! He is giving us extra fireworks. He is saying Happy happy wedding day!

CHRIS. Fuck around in my house of worship and I'll throw a bolt in your head. Is what he's saying.

ADIEL. Ag he did not bring us together to throw a bolt in our heads.

CHRIS. Yeh. Well. We won't know till we know will we?

ADIEL. Chris. What is the matter?

CHRIS. Nothing. Just, thunderstorms. I don't like them.
(Re: church.) This, is beautiful. When did you have the time to set all this up?

ADIEL. You were late.

CHRIS. Candles…flowers…a, Oreo?

ADIEL. Ah that one is a gift. From Francis.

CHRIS. Francis? The guy who's crushing on you?

ADIEL. No, that is Philip. Francis is my cousin who is crushing on You.

CHRIS. You brought me a cookie from your com…

ADIEL. The competition is eight years old and he really wanted you to have this one. I am not worried. Very soon you belong only to me.

tart

(ADIEL *holds out her palms.*)

CHRIS. What?

ADIEL. The rings?

CHRIS. Oh. Um.

ADIEL. What?

CHRIS. …

ADIEL. Ag Chris, that was the one thing you were in charge of.

CHRIS. I'm sorry. My parents, found them and, took them.

ADIEL. Your parents? Why?

CHRIS. Because. For safekeeping. They're paranoid, since the news up north. The whole town's so paranoid, it's contagious. Can't wait to get out of this place where we can live like normal people.

ADIEL. This place is my home.

CHRIS. It doesn't always have to be.

ADIEL. Christina I do not want to argue about that right now.

CHRIS. Don't call me Christina.

I wanted everything to be perfect too. I wanted rings. Champagne. Sunlight.

ADIEL. We have candlelight. And here a ring. For now.

(*The strip of aluminum from the bottle cap –* ADIEL *twists it into a pretty ring.*)

CHRIS. I knew this boy back home. He'd always play with wires, bend them into goats – sometimes other things but mostly goats, he loved goats – goat tribes, goat battle scenes, little goat armies lined up and at attention. He had no friends and was bullied a lot but then one of the teachers found his goats, and helped him apply to this arts school in Colorado, all for free, even the plane ticket. You know what I mean?

ADIEL. No.

CHRIS. I'm saying, you could probably do something like that.

ADIEL. You want that I make armies of wire goats?

CHRIS. No, I want that you apply to a school in America. You can make pretty things. You can go to school for free if you can make pretty things in my country, learn to make more pretty things, sell them, buy a car, buy a boat, a plane, an army of wire goats –

ADIEL. Chris. If you are making stupid jokes because you do not want to do this, tell me right now.

CHRIS. I do. I do want to. I'm sorry. Don't be angry.

ADIEL. I am not angry. Just making sure.

CHRIS. I am sure.

(ADIEL *makes sure.*)

ADIEL. We have everything else, candle, cookie, tape recorder –

CHRIS. Tape recorder?

ADIEL. Because we do not have witnesses, we must record the vows, so when you are mine, you are mine forever.

CHRIS. This isn't legal or anything, I can crush the records and run away whenever I like.

ADIEL. But I will hunt you down to the ends of the earth. I will hunt you down forever. Forever forever I will say, "Come back to meeeeeeeeee come back to me my husbaaaaaaaaaand come back to meeeeeeeeeeeeeeeeeeee I have this tape recordeerrrrrrrrrrrr."

CHRIS. Okay let's do it.

(ADIEL *pulls out a couple of neatly composed handwritten documents.*)

ADIEL. Number one, you must say this, with your name in there, and then I say the same, with My name not yours of course.

CHRIS. Wow. You are not joking around.

ADIEL. I never joke. Number two, You do the ring and say this part. Unless you want to be the bride, then I do the ring to you, and I say this part.

CHRIS. Wait, where'd you get this stuff from?

ADIEL. From our pastor.

(CHRIS *takes a pen to* ADIEL*'s vow papers.*)

CHRIS. Okay, strike "lawful," strike "according to God's holy ordinance," / and strike the second part of this whole section –

ADIEL. AH! What are you doing, you are ruining the vow papers!

CHRIS. – we are not endowing anything in the name of the father the son or the holy ghost. Because they don't care. Amen should go too.

ADIEL. We must do the whole vow.

CHRIS. No we don't. It's our wedding we can do whatever we want.

ADIEL. Well that is not what I want.

(ADIEL *clicks "rec" button on the tape recorder.*)

This is the wedding of Christina Jennifer Englewood and Adiel Nakalinzi. January 1st, year 2000.

(*She gestures to* CHRIS: *"Go ahead, begin the vows."*)

CHRIS. What? Oh okay, me first. I, Chris Blank, take thee,

(ADIEL *hits stop.*)

ADIEL. What are you doing.

CHRIS. I'm gonna find another name. I've disowned my parents.

ADIEL. What does that mean? Shoo, you are making this impossible,

You have to have whole name, say I, Christina Jennifer Engelwood. Start again.

(Rewind. Rec.)

ADIEL. This is the wedding of Christina Jennifer Englewood and Adiel Nakalinzi. January 1st, year 2000.

CHRIS. I, Chris Blank, take thee, Adiel Nakalinzi, to be my wife, ugh, that's such a dumb word.

(**ADIEL** hits stop.)

ADIEL. Chris!

(**CHRIS** takes the recorder. Rec.)

CHRIS. To be my wife, to have and to hold from this day forward, for better for worse for richer for poorer in sickness and in health to love and to cherish till death do us part, according to, I don't know, according to this dimly lit candle's holy ordinance, and thereto I give thee my troth. What's a troth? Sounds slimy.

ADIEL. I, Adiel Nakalinzi, take thee, Christina Jennifer Englewood,

CHRIS. Chris Blank

ADIEL. Christina Jennifer Englewood, to be my lawful wedded husband, to have and –

(**CHRIS** hits stop.)

CHRIS. Stop right there, I refuse to be a husband in this life or the next, do over.

ADIEL. What, we have two wives then? That is a house of widows.

CHRIS. I don't care, make it work, not gonna be a husband. Ew.

ADIEL. A sad grieving house of sad sad widows.

(Sad face.)

CHRIS. Ugh.

(**ADIEL** hits rec.)

ADIEL. I, Adiel Nakalinzi, take thee, Christina Jennifer Englewood, to be my lawful wedded Husband,

(**CHRIS** *leans into mic on recorder.*)

CHRIS. Ugh.

ADIEL. – to have and to hold from this day, forward, for better for worse, for richer for poorer, in sickness and in health, to love and to cherish, till death us do part, according to God's holy ordinance; and thereto I plight thee my troth.

CHRIS. With this ring I thee wed, with my body I thee worship, and with all my worldly goods I thee endow.

ADIEL. In the name of.

CHRIS. In the name of the Father, and of the Son, and of the Holy Ghost. Amen.

ADIEL. Amen. Now I may kiss the husband.

> (*Kiss. With all the nerves and rituals of the Newlyweds' First Kiss.*)

Now we must dance.

CHRIS. No. We must not.

> (**ADIEL** *begins to sing "Unchained Melody"*** *by The Righteous Brothers.* **CHRIS** *laughs out loud at the song choice, but soon surrenders to* **ADIEL**'s *insistence.*)

CHRIS. Seriously?

ADIEL. Yes.

> (**ADIEL** *continues to sing, pulling* **CHRIS** *into the performance.*)
>
> (*They dance together, like people in love, soaking in the cheese and tender, all of it.*)

**A license to produce *Cardboard Piano* does not include a performance license for "Unchained Melody." The publisher and author suggest that the licensee contact ASCAP or BMI to ascertain the music publisher and contact such music publisher to license or acquire permission for performance of the song. If a license or permission is unattainable for "Unchained Melody," the licensee may not use the song in *Carboard Piano* but may create an original composition in a similar style. For further information, please see Music Use Note on page 3.

(Just as they're about to reach the end of the second verse, a noise.)

(!!)

(Scuffling of feet on dirt, random shouts, coming from outside.)

CHRIS. What's the time?

ADIEL. After midnight at the very least.

CHRIS. It must be people getting out from the party. Blow them out, the candles!

(Silence.)

(Then doors opening, slamming, feet shuffling on dirt, whispered sounds.)

ADIEL. Did you lock the door?

CHRIS. I'm getting it now

*(Bang, gunshots. **CHRIS** and **ADIEL** duck.)*

Jesus!

ADIEL. Chris!

CHRIS. It's alright I'm fine are you? Are you okay?

ADIEL. Get over here, get over here right now!

CHRIS. I know, okay I'm [gonna lock the door first].

*(Door opens, **PIKA** leaps in, grabs **CHRIS**, hand over mouth.)*

PIKA. Shh!

*(Points bloody gun toward **ADIEL**, then to **CHRIS'** head.)*

*(Motions to **CHRIS** to lock the door. She does.)*

(More footsteps, pad pad pad past the door, and away.)

(Wait wait.)

(Wait wait.)

(Wait wait.)

*(**PIKA** leans against a wall, exhausted, out of breath, faints.)*

> *(CHRIS leaps back away from him. ADIEL leaps forward toward CHRIS.)*

ADIEL. Are you okay.

CHRIS. Mm. [yes]

ADIEL. Did he hurt you? Any –

CHRIS. Mm-mm. [no]

ADIEL. Okay good okay. Hold on.

> *(Checks pulse. Breath.)*

CHRIS. Is he [dead]?

ADIEL. He's okay.

> *(CHRIS looks for a rope-type thing.)*
>
> *(ADIEL pries gun from PIKA, wipes the blood off. CHRIS has found a rope-type thing, gives it to ADIEL.)*

What?

CHRIS. For [tying him up].

> *(ADIEL hands gun to CHRIS while she ties up PIKA.)*

ADIEL. Okay.

CHRIS. Okay.

ADIEL. Sit there take a breath / and I will go bring your parents.

CHRIS. Okay.

My –

ADIEL. You said they were still here, right? They did not go to New Year Party.

CHRIS. No.

ADIEL. So I will bring them down.

CHRIS. You can't. You can't bring them. You can't wake them up.

ADIEL. Chris we must. That child is hurt.

CHRIS. You can't.

ADIEL. He cannot do anything to us now, I promise.

CHRIS. No it's not that.

ADIEL. What is it then?

CHRIS. You can't call them.

ADIEL. We need a grown up, Christina. That child needs help.

CHRIS. That child tried to kill me.

ADIEL. He was only asking for help. He –

CHRIS. He tried to kill me.

ADIEL. He is a rebel soldier, he is hurt. He needs bandage, doctor, do you understand Christina, if we do not wake up your parents that boy might die while we watch.

CHRIS. We can't.

ADIEL. I will not argue about this

CHRIS. No we seriously can't, they won't wake up. They won't wake up, Adiel, I –
I drugged them.

ADIEL. What?

CHRIS. Sleeping pills. In the tea, not very much just, two more than what they usually take,

ADIEL. You did what?!

CHRIS. I needed the car keys. He sleeps with them Velcroed in his pockets, I didn't know how else to –

ADIEL. Every time? Every time we met, you were poisoning our pastor?

CHRIS. It's not poison! And of course not every time, just tonight, I needed the keys, time to pack and –
Look, I think there's a first aid kit in the office,

ADIEL. Pack?

CHRIS. We have to leave tonight. I have everything we need here, in this bag,
I meant to tell you as soon as –, but you were so cute and happy and the vows and song, I didn't want to ruin, I wanted to get through the –

ADIEL. What are you saying?

CHRIS. Escape.

ADIEL. Escape.

CHRIS. We have to escape. This this place, this prison of –

ADIEL. We are in a church Chris.

CHRIS. I mean metaphorically.

ADIEL. So, escape metaphorically?

CHRIS. No that part is real. The prison is metaphor, the escape is real.

ADIEL. You are muddling my brain, there's a boy bleeding over here,

CHRIS. We'll fix it. We can fix it, we'll find the first aid kit, fix the guy who tried to kill me, then we'll get in the car drive to the check point –

ADIEL. Get in the car and drive to the – you can hardly find the way to the bus stop, how –

CHRIS. We'll figure it out!

ADIEL. Why?!

CHRIS. They know. My parents. They know.

ADIEL. About –

CHRIS. Us.

ADIEL. Ha.

CHRIS. Yep.

ADIEL. How?

CHRIS. The rings. I had our names written on the inside, as a surprise for you,

She asked about – so I told.

ADIEL. And?

CHRIS. They didn't.

ADIEL. Of course not! Why did you / do this, this this –

CHRIS. It's not safe, not safe here anymore, I couldn't just / leave, didn't know if –

ADIEL. Without even one word / to me, did you,

CHRIS. I thought they might take you too, if I, for us, oh come / on, Adiel,

ADIEL. My auntie is going to have me killed. Killed, Christina, did you even think about that what it means to me if the people here find out do you know what that means for me?

CHRIS. It won't mean anything, because we are going to live in Tunisia.

ADIEL. Tunisia?

CHRIS. We'll patch up the kid, pack up the car, and drive past the checkpoint, you can hide in the trunk till we get to the border –

ADIEL. You, are the missionary pastor's daughter!

Missionary pastor's daughters do not do this way, poison their parents and then run away to –

CHRIS. They're leaving. Moving boxes, plane tickets, really leaving Adiel. With me.

I had to tell them, they are these people who are supposed to love me the most in the world

I thought maybe they would, understand, thought they'd –

But it went wrong, okay, it just went wrong and –

ADIEL. So we must go to Tunisia?

CHRIS. Adiel if we are gonna do this, each other is all we're gonna have left, we have to put everything on the line. I mean EVERYTHING. I have to put my God on the altar, you have to put your country on the altar, and say, none of these things matter more to us than each other, each other is our everything, for each other we are willing to burn them destroy them / to to to give them up –

ADIEL. Chris you are not making any sense,

CHRIS. Whatever "them" is for either of us. You know that game, that game where they ask you, if you were stranded on an island, and you get to take just the one thing, what would you take? Except it's not a game, we Are stranded on an island, we are all stranded on an island on our own, and we get to choose one thing just the one thing that we will carry with us always.

My parents chose God your parents chose country and look what happened to them! Mine are forced to box up their house and dreams in a weekend, yours are dead.

I can't do that, I can't be stranded on an island on my own, I Choose You. But it only works if you choose me too.

ADIEL. So you poisoned them?

CHRIS. Adiel!

ADIEL. This is too much Chris.

CHRIS. They were making me leave you.

ADIEL. We had a plan, we were getting married –

CHRIS. That's not a real plan! What's the point of getting married when I'm eight thousand miles away –

> (**PIKA** *comes to, finds his bearings, discovers bondage. Frantic, he tries to grab his pocket knife to undo bondage. Girls lunge away from him.*)

Get in, get in, back of the,

PIKA. Let me go.

ADIEL. We are here to help.

CHRIS. Adiel!

PIKA. You tied me up.

ADIEL. You were being difficult at first. Look. Medicine. For you.

PIKA. Stay there. Let me see inside the box first.

ADIEL. See, just bandages and ice packs.

CHRIS. I say we go inside the office and lock the door.

ADIEL. You do that if you want to.

PIKA. They cut off my ear.

ADIEL. Yes, I know.

CHRIS. Adiel this is not safe.

ADIEL. You are bleeding. We can help you stop the blood. Can I come closer? We can help you.

> (**PIKA** *lowers the blade.*)

Can you put that down please?

> (**PIKA** *puts the blade down. Close, though.*)

Thank you. I am Adiel. What is your name?

PIKA. Pika.

ADIEL. Okay Pika, let us sit you up, can you lean your head this way, good. You must not lie down, okay?

> (**ADIEL** *unties him.*)

CHRIS. Adiel what are you insane?

ADIEL. You poison your parents and I am insane?

CHRIS. This is a bad idea. Worse than my Tunisia idea, in fact, we won't have to go to Tunisia, because we will be dead anyway.

ADIEL. Come here.

CHRIS. Dead!

ADIEL. Chris I need your help, come here.

CHRIS. Dead.

ADIEL. Stop saying dead and keep this rag on his head. You must apply pressure, we cannot do anything until he stops bleeding.

We cannot go to Tunisia until he stops bleeding.

> (**CHRIS** *reluctantly goes to* **ADIEL** *and the boy.*)
>
> (*Takes over the rags.*)

CHRIS. Oh god oh jesus this is oh wow.

ADIEL. You can put more pressure, you must be firm.

CHRIS. How do you know all this.

ADIEL. In my country, you have to learn to do more than just make pretty things.

CHRIS. That's why I'm saying, we should go to Tunisia. Where are you going!

ADIEL. To get water!

CHRIS. Come back here. Come back here! Adiel, get back here right –

> (*She's gone.*)
>
> (*Silence.*)

Let's just, get this…

(**CHRIS** *pushes the blade away kinda sorta subtly,*
PIKA *is rigid.*)

No, I'm not gonna, I just wanted to,

(*The blade is out of easy reach.*)

I'm Chris.

PIKA. Yes.

CHRIS. What happened? Your *[gestures, ear]*, I mean you
don't have to say if you don't want to –

PIKA. I tried to run away and then he catch me and then I
run away again.

CHRIS. Does it hurt?

Do you want something? Lemonade?

Or, Oreo?

(**PIKA** *stares at the Oreo for a bit before taking it.*)

(*He eats the Oreo in silence.*)

PIKA. There is a hole in the roof.

CHRIS. Yep.

PIKA. What happened?

CHRIS. Don't know. We woke up one morning and there
was this dead bird on the pews, and a hole in the roof
above it. I like it, kinda like a skylight. Lets the breeze
in, and you can see the stars in the night,

(**ADIEL**'s *back with a bucket of water.*)

ADIEL. How are we doing?

CHRIS. Great.

(*She checks beneath the rag.*)

ADIEL. Little bit longer.

(**ADIEL** *preps the bandages, alcohol swabs.*)

PIKA. I like it too. The people in this church can pray, see
God directly, and pray.

ADIEL. Hm?

CHRIS. The hole. He likes the hole in our roof.

ADIEL. Do you like to pray?

PIKA. The Commander, he makes us pray very very much. In the morning, in the night, the other children, they are not so committed. I am committed. But I want to look at the sky when I am talking to God. Not to close my eyes, or bow my head like the Commander wants.

CHRIS. What do you pray about?

ADIEL. You can let go now.

> (CHRIS *lets go.* ADIEL *wets the rag, cleans the clots of blood around his lobbed-off ear.*)

PIKA. My soul.

CHRIS. Your soul?

PIKA. I pray for my soul. I have done many bad things.

ADIEL. Now this will hurt a little, hold on to Chris if you want to.

> (*He does.*)
>
> (*Alcohol swabs. Dab dab, while blowing gently, wince wince.*)

Good boy, almost finished. Good boy.

PIKA. I am not a good boy.

ADIEL. No? Chris can you help me cut this tape.

CHRIS. Yeah. Of course.

PIKA. In the bush, I dream, my soul is shrinking, like a little raisin, tiny like one rain,
and it disappears away into the ocean. God does not hear me in this ocean. I do not hear Him.

ADIEL. Well you are not in the bush, you are not in the ocean, you are here with us, in our church. And He is very happy you are here, Pika.

PIKA. No. I am lost. I am surrounded by bad souls and I cannot breathe cannot remember who I am and now I am also bad soul. I am a very bad soul and cannot remember how to pray I cannot remember His voice I cannot remember how to talk to him. I am a terrible bad soul and so He has forgotten about me. He has forgotten.

(**PIKA** *cries, and cries. Cries like a thirteen-year-old boy cries when he is very scared.*)

(*He cries, and cries.*)

CHRIS. Pika how old are you?

PIKA. Thirteen.

CHRIS. Okay, so when I was a kid, even younger than you, I had this thing about a piano. Obsession.

One day, my dad's like, Chris, I got a surprise for you, I'm like, IT'S A PIANO. He reaches behind and gives me, well, he's cut out a cereal box, and built a small piano out of the cardboard.

He plays, singing the notes he's playing, like,

"doon doon doon doon doon doon doon doon,"

what do I do? I snatch it, tear it all up.

Soon as I did it I knew I did something bad, because the look on his face was –

And I watch him pick up the pieces, go to his office, close the door.

I'm thinking, he's gone. He hates me. He'll forget me and find another daughter in my place,

Finally I can't take it anymore so I go knock on his door, crying Daddy I'm sorry.

Door opens, and you know what I see? The piano.

He's been in there this whole time, putting the piano back together.

He goes, "doon doon doon doon doon doon doon," and while I'm crying snot and tears, he lifts me onto his lap, says, "Chris, this is all we have, for now. It's small and fragile, so easy to break.

But look, I fixed it.

Every time we break something, it's okay, long as we fix it. And I did. So it's okay."

(*The boy has stopped crying.*)

PIKA. That is the most bad thing that you did?

CHRIS. Ha. No. I wish.

PIKA. I do not know how to fix my soul.

CHRIS. Maybe someone else is fixing it, you just can't see yet.

> (CHRIS *finds a blanket or throw, wraps it around the boy.*)
>
> (ADIEL *activates an ice pack and places it on his wound.*)

ADIEL. Here, this is cold, press it to your bandages, yes like that. The blood is not completely stopped, so you must not lie down yet, alright?

PIKA. Thank you.

> (ADIEL *waits for* PIKA *to settle, and then takes* CHRIS *aside.*)

ADIEL. If we go, you might never see your father again.

CHRIS. I know.

ADIEL. You might never be able to fix it, with either of them.

CHRIS. I know.

ADIEL. Once we leave, we cannot return. We cannot undo what we are about to do. Do you understand this?

CHRIS. Adiel, once I get on that plane with them I cannot come back.

ADIEL. Okay.

CHRIS. !

ADIEL. Not Tunisia. We can go down to the city. It will be easy for us to find something to do in the city. Much easier than me trying to cross the borders without a passport.

CHRIS. Great. Yes. Okay.

ADIEL. First I must go home.

CHRIS. What? No.

ADIEL. I cannot just leave,

CHRIS. I don't think it's safe to be outside right now,

ADIEL. I have to let them know that I am leaving, not, Taken,

CHRIS. We could leave them a note, here?

ADIEL. My auntie will be very heartbroken, she must be allowed to be so, in private.

CHRIS. I'll come with.

ADIEL. No.

CHRIS. I don't think this is a good idea Adiel.

ADIEL. I know this town. The shadows, the paths. I'll be fine.

(**CHRIS** *takes the gun from where it was hidden.*)

CHRIS. Take this.

ADIEL. Chris –

CHRIS. Just, in case. Please be careful.

Start

(**ADIEL** *leaves. With gun.*)

PIKA. You are leaving?

CHRIS. Yeah. Do you think she'll be okay?

PIKA. Why are you leaving? Is this a bad township?

CHRIS. No. No, it's pretty great, nice township – the men that you were running from, they've gone? You think?

PIKA. Maybe. Are you running away too?

CHRIS. Kind of.

PIKA. You do something bad?

CHRIS. No. Yes, maybe, I don't know, depends on what you decide is bad.

PIKA. I did something bad. I did many things bad. I do not want more bad things, so I run away. They catch me, but then I run away again. If they catch me again, I will be like meerkat –

(**PIKA** *does an unexpected impression of a meerkat.*)

– two big black holes at the side of the head.

CHRIS. Oh.

PIKA. You said you are going to the city.

CHRIS. Yes.

PIKA. Can I come with?

CHRIS. With us? Huh, wow, I don't know, Pika.

PIKA. If I stay in this township, or alone somewhere else, they will find me. And then I become meerkat. Or maybe they kill me. Mostly they kill second time finds.

CHRIS. Where's your home? Wouldn't it be better to go home?

PIKA. I do not remember, I was taken when I was ten. Three years ago. Even if I do find my home again, my family will not want me because I am bad.

CHRIS. Look, that's tough, but –

PIKA. If I am with other people who are family, they cannot make advance.

CHRIS. We aren't your family.

PIKA. I can help with many things. I am trained for battle I can steal foods or climb over walls and trees I can defend you and your friend Adiel. I can do many many things. If you are worried about my bad soul, I promise you I will fix it.

CHRIS. How do you fix a bad soul?

I mean, it's not about your soul, good or bad, it's just, we don't know each other, we can't just start living together. Maybe if you stay here, talk to my dad in the morning, he might help you out, but maybe not, our pastor won't be in such a soul fixing mood after his only child runs away.

PIKA. Your dad is the pastor?

CHRIS. Yup.

PIKA. Why are you running away? All your problems can be solved here.

CHRIS. Yeah, no. Look, I don't know how God or pastors do it, but I know how the real world does it.

PIKA. Do what?

CHRIS. Fix your soul.

PIKA. The real world has powers to fix the soul?

CHRIS. Sure.

PIKA. Who is the real world?

CHRIS. You know, countries, governments, people. In South Africa, they had a truth and reconciliation committee, they made it international, everyone could tap in on the hearings. It was super successful and nearly everyone's souls were fixed. The president won the Nobel Peace Prize for it.

PIKA. How is it done? Do you know how to do it?

CHRIS. Sure. It's not that hard. It's just some people listening to other people after a time of, bad things, and then, for the criminals – deciding whether or not to forgive, for the victims – deciding how to rehabilitate, restore, make better. They also decided who were the criminals who were the victims.

PIKA. Who has the power to decide?

CHRIS. The people.

PIKA. There is just two of us.

CHRIS. So I will be the people. And we can put your hearing on tape, and if we find more people, they can weigh in.

PIKA. I don't understand why you have the power.

CHRIS. Me neither, but it seemed to have worked for them, it's worth a shot? I mean, I am the pastor's kid so maybe I can gather forces from the real world and the God world.

PIKA. I did many bad things.

CHRIS. Here, put your right hand on this bible.

PIKA. More bad than breaking a piano.

CHRIS. Come on, can't hurt to try?

> (*He does.*)
>
> (**CHRIS** *hits rec.*)

End

CHRIS. Do you, Pika the ex-soldier, solemnly swear to tell the whole truth and nothing but the truth so help you God.

PIKA. Okay.

CHRIS. It is January 1st, year 2000, we are gathered here today for the public hearing of ex-soldier Pika, who has applied for absolution from the bad things of his past. My name is Christina Jennifer Englewood and I will be representing the people. Pika, tell us what you have done.

PIKA. Everything?

CHRIS. Everything.

PIKA. I cannot remember everything. It is very very long list.

CHRIS. Then pick one of the worst.

PIKA. I do not want to tell. You would not like me. You would not want to take me with you.

CHRIS. Pika we're doing this so we might be able to.

PIKA. Okay.

CHRIS. Go on.

PIKA. There was a man, he was a soldier of the army too. He was high ranks, he ate with the Commander but he was discovered, of helping girls escape the army. The man was tied up to a tree. The Commander called some names, and each soldier whose name was called must come and cut a piece of the man off with the machete while the man was still alive. When My name was called, there was not very much left to cut off so the Commander order me to cut off the head. I did. It was not easy because I was still new and did not have strength with machete. And then after I cut off the head the Commander order me to throw the head in the air and catch it three times, like this, like this, like this. And then kick it like a soccer ball like this. Then we sing the song,

Polo polo yesu olara, eh.

Yesu olara woko ki ii bal

Aye tiyo tic pa lala ii kwo wa ii to.

His head roll on to the road, that is where we left it.

CHRIS. Wow.

PIKA. Do you hate me now?

CHRIS. No.

PIKA. Do you think it worked?

CHRIS. How do you feel?

PIKA. Terrible.

CHRIS. It is the decision of the people to grant absolution to ex-soldier Pika. May your soul find peace in this court's ruling. How about now?

PIKA. A little better. Does that mean I can come with you?

>   (**CHRIS** *gets close to the mic on the tape recorder.*)

CHRIS. Yes.

PIKA. Yes?!

CHRIS. We have to talk to Adiel, but, she's the easy one.

>   (**CHRIS** *takes out cassette and presents it to* **PIKA**.)

PIKA. Thank you. Thank you.

>   (*Hugs.*)

CHRIS. Yay family!

>   (**CHRIS** *blows on her blower: Yes!*)

>   (**PIKA** *grabs the blower and flings it away.*)

PIKA. What is that!

CHRIS. I'm sorry,

PIKA. They will come here. Why did you do that! / They will come here.

CHRIS. Sorry I wasn't – It's been a while, your people have probably left. Adiel went out on her own, there's no way she would've gone outside if she thought they were still –

>   (*Someone rattles the door.*)

CHRIS. That's Adi –

>   (**PIKA** *yanks her down.*)

>   (*Finger to his lips, and creeps along toward the window, takes a peek.*)

(*He sees.*)

Who –

(**PIKA***'s frightened eyes shuts her up.*)

(*They look for a place to hide.*)

(*More sounds, door rattle.*)

(**CHRIS** *gestures up there!*)

(*They climb up onto the roof.*)

(*Door is knocked in.*)

(*A* **SOLDIER** *enters.*)

SOLDIER. Pika…

(**SOLDIER** *looks around.*)

Pika…?

(**SOLDIER** *notices the bloody rags, water.*)

Pika. You know there is nowhere to go. Nobody else wants you. Come now. Let us go home.

Nobody needs to know about our adventure tonight, it'll be our little secret, eh?

(*Hurried footsteps come closer.*)

CHRIS. Adiel!

(**PIKA** *shushes her, holds her back, shakes his head.*)

(**ADIEL** *runs in through the broken doorway.*)

(*She stops dead in her tracks when she sees the* **SOLDIER**.)

SOLDIER. Hello.

ADIEL. If you were looking for shelter, there was no need to break the door. The house of our Lord is always open.

SOLDIER. This one was closed and locked.

(**SOLDIER** *holds up the bloody rag.*)

I am looking for a lost soldier. I think he is here?

ADIEL. I don't know. I hope you find what you are looking for.

(SOLDIER blocks her path.)

I was simply passing by and I saw the broken door.

SOLDIER. I see.

ADIEL. Goodnight.

SOLDIER. Where are you going so late in the night?

ADIEL. Just out for a walk.

SOLDIER. With a travel bag?

ADIEL. Yes.

SOLDIER. Running away, like my lost soldier? Or even With my lost soldier?

ADIEL. Just out for a walk.

SOLDIER. I see. We are going to make this a game.

> *(SOLDIER takes out a weapon, probably a machete.)*

CHRIS. Fuck, no,

PIKA. Shh!

SOLDIER. I do not like games.

> *(PIKA starts to climb down the side of the wall – outside.)*

CHRIS. What are you doing!

> *(PIKA shushes her violently.)*

SOLDIER. I ask again. I am looking for a lost soldier.

ADIEL. I think I am looking at one.

SOLDIER. You think you are? How old are you?

ADIEL. Twenty. Five.

SOLDIER. Are you lying?

ADIEL. No.

SOLDIER. That is unfortunate. If you were younger I could take you with me. Now I have to kill you.
It's a joke.

> *(PIKA appears in the window or doorway, so that ADIEL spots him.)*
>
> *(He gestures: roof.)*

I don't like to kill beautiful girls. If I can help it.

So last chance. Where is Pika.

> (**CHRIS** *starts climbing down the way* **PIKA** *went.*)
>
> (*A slip,* **CHRIS** *makes a sound.*)
>
> (**SOLDIER** *hears, turns toward the sound with his machete —*)

ADIEL. He left.

SOLDIER. What?

ADIEL. I saw him outside the window just a few moments ago.

> (**SOLDIER** *starts to leave.*)
>
> (**PIKA** *leaps into the shadows.*)

Let him go. He is poisoned. Broken. He does not care about this country.

I do. Let me come with you.

SOLDIER. You want to come with me?

ADIEL. I want to help, take care of you.

SOLDIER. You want to take care of me?

ADIEL. Yes.

> (**PIKA** *climbs back up to the roof.*)

SOLDIER. Whoever has taught you how to lie, has done a very good job.

ADIEL. Or maybe I am not lying.

> (**ADIEL** *undoes his buckle.*)
>
> (**PIKA** *re-appears to* **CHRIS**.)

PIKA. Psst. Psst!

> (*He has a rock. She helps.*)

SOLDIER. You are a strange little girl.

ADIEL. Is it so strange to be attracted to a powerful man?

SOLDIER. You are attracted to me?

ADIEL. Yes.

> (*Her hands in his pants.*)

(**SOLDIER**'s *hands slide where she has hidden the gun.*)

No. Not yet. Down there.

SOLDIER. Giving orders already

(**SOLDIER** *finds the gun on* **ADIEL**.)

What is –

Ha.

Good game soldier.

ADIEL. It's not mine. I forgot it was even there / I promise you.

SOLDIER. Were you going to shoot me?

ADIEL. No no of course not.

(*Sudden movement, soldier leaps toward* **ADIEL**, **PIKA** *falls on top of the man with the rock aimed for his head.*)

PIKA. AAAAAAAAAAH!

(*Bam.*)

SOLDIER. Wha – What is, you –

(**PIKA** *bashes in the skull of the soldier, repeatedly.*)

(*Bambam bambam bambambambam –*)

(*Stands back.*)

(*Is he dead?*)

(*Absolute Stillness.*)

(**CHRIS** *is the first to move [on the roof].*)

(**ADIEL** *and* **PIKA** *start.*)

CHRIS. It's me, just me. Chris.

ADIEL. Chris.

CHRIS. I'm so sorry. I'm so sorry. Imsosorrysosorry.

ADIEL. I thought you were, / I didn't know,

CHRIS. I wanted to but / I couldn't,

ADIEL. Pika?

PIKA. I am okay.

ADIEL. I thought you were, I didn't know what / you were, where,

CHRIS. You were so brave, so brave, I'm so / sorry Adiel I didn't know what to, Pika, and –

> (**CHRIS** *embraces* **ADIEL**.)

ADIEL. It's okay, I understand. Everything's alright, it's alright. Shh…

> (**CHRIS** *kisses* **ADIEL** *like life and death.*)

PIKA. What are you doing.

ADIEL. Pika.

PIKA. What were you, you were, you were doing like a man and his wife.

CHRIS. She Is my wife.

ADIEL. Chris don't –

PIKA. That is a sin and abomination and evil in the sight of God. God has saved your life tonight, God has saved three of our lives tonight and in his house you will make sin, dirty in sin.

ADIEL. Pika,

PIKA. Do not touch me you are a filthy sinner dirty sinner abomination.

> (**PIKA** *grabs a gun.*)

ADIEL. Pika that is not what God wants.

> (*Bang.*)

PIKA. You do not know what God wants.

> (**ADIEL** *falls.*)

CHRIS. No.

No no no no no

What did you do. What is, What was – What's going on I don't,

Adiel look at me, hey, look, up here, come on Adiel.

Adiel! Adiel please look at me please please look at me Adiel.

(**PIKA** *gets closer to* **ADIEL**.)

Don't you fucking dare.

(**CHRIS** *gets gun.*)

PIKA. I can help, let me.

(*Bang. She missed.*)

Chris. Please I –

(*Bang. She missed.*)

(*Bang bang bang Bang bang bang Bang bang bang Bang bang bang.*)

(**PIKA** *has run out during the bangs.*)

(**CHRIS** *still shoots, without ammo.*)

(*Bang bang bang click click click click.*)

(**CHRIS** *alone with* **ADIEL** *in the church.*)

(**PIKA** *alone with himself, somewhere else.*)

POLO POLO YESU OLARA, EH.
YESU OLARA WOKO KI II BAL
AYE TIYO TIC PA LALA II KWO WA II TO.
POLO POLO YESU OLARA, EH.
YESU OLARA WOKO KI II BAL
AYE TIYO TIC PA LALA II KWO WA II TO.

(*A very angry, sad battle cry.*)

(*Whose?*)

End of Part I

PART II

*(The ensemble minus **CHRIS**.)*

(A single, tentative voice, gradually grows into more sound, more joy.)

ALL BUT CHRIS.

POLO POLO YESU OLARA, EH.
YESU OLARA WOKO KI II BAL
AYE TIYO TIC PA LALA II KWO WA II TO.
POLO POLO YESU OLARA, EH.
YESU OLARA WOKO KI II BAL
AYE TIYO TIC PA LALA II KWO WA II TO.
POLO POLO YESU OLARA, EH.
YESU OLARA WOKO KI II BAL
AYE TIYO TIC PA LALA II KWO WA II TO.

(Day.)

(The church is the same church, only cleaner, more modern. It is a beautiful church; a lot of it has changed, but it somehow feels the same. The hole in the roof is now replaced with a skylight, while the space is decorated with wild flowers.)

(And somewhere, a tea set. The tea in the pot has gone cold.)

PAUL. "Everybody knows, in this story, the traveler is met with some ill fate. He is beaten, robbed, and then left half dead along the road. He is lying in the ditch bleeding to his death. Not long before first the priest, somebody like me, he passes by, sees the man in pain! Will he save him? No. He takes off. Second the Levite, somebody like our deacon Abuu, he passes by and sees the man in pain! Will he save him? No he is going off as well. Third the Samaritan, somebody like the political

38

criminal, somebody that we all hate all together, somebody we believe is a bad man, he passes by. And boom, he of course, helps the dying traveler.

And we all think about this little story, that it is a teaching about kindness.

About moral and ethical responsibility. About being nice. But, really? Is Jesus spending all this creative energy to tell us to be nice? Come on now, we know, we know we must be nice. Not just those of faith, but everybody knows this, if you are a person, you know that it is a good thing to try and be nice to another person, especially if that person is naked and bleeding at the side of the road.

To understand what Jesus is really talking about, we must understand that this story is an answer to a question asked by some scholar in the crowd. The scholar asks the question, who is this "neighbor" that we must love. In fact, what is love?

Is love a feeling? A sensual pull toward one certain human being?

A little chemical released into our bodies that drains the brain of oxygen, and pumps the heart like the phone on vibration, so that all of your blood flows, races through all the veins in your body, makes you think about that person only, is that love? If that is love, I do not know if my wife will appreciate Jesus asking me to love all my neighbors so much."

(*He laughs at his joke.*)

(**RUTH** *has entered at some point.*)

That is a good joke. Let me write this one down.

RUTH. I don't get the joke.

PAUL. Ruth!

RUTH. Why am I in your sermon as a joke?

PAUL. What happened? Do you know what time it is?

RUTH. Ai yai, you know, I met somebody on the street, Pastor –

PAUL. You met somebody on the street is why you are so late for our date?

RUTH. A date? African husbands do not date their African wives.

PAUL. This African husband does. Who did you meet?

RUTH. What is this! Tea? You made tea! And flowers. This man has stolen all the flowers of Africa to put them in our church.

PAUL. The aunties of the congregation brought them over for our celebration. I just bunched them artfully and placed them around the church. For our tea.

RUTH. You are very proud of your tea.

PAUL. And my flowers.

RUTH. So many flowers.

PAUL. I was inspired.

RUTH. Yes?

PAUL. Yes, by a beautiful lady with the regretful habit of forgetting the time on her wedding anniversary.

RUTH. It is only our second one. I have to do it more than three times for it to be a habit.

PAUL. So next year it will be a habit.

RUTH. Ah, already you are giving up on me?

PAUL. Never. Pastor is not allowed to give up on members of his church. Not even his wife.

Come. Sit. Let us have some very old very lukewarm tea.

(They sit. He pours the tea in each cup.)

RUTH. Thank you.

PAUL. Okay so you sit there, and I will –

RUTH. Where are you going?

PAUL. I am going to give you my wedding anniversary gift.

RUTH. What? Pastor, we agreed we are not giving gifts this year.

PAUL. I know, but I had a very good idea for a gift. Here is your bible.

(He goes to the pulpit.)

Now let us turn to the Gospel of Luke chapter ten verses twenty-five to thirty-seven.

RUTH. Pastor what are you doing?

PAUL. I am giving you a sermon.

RUTH. Your anniversary gift is a sermon?

PAUL. Yes.

RUTH. Your very good idea of a gift is to make me sit still and listen to you practicing your sermon.

PAUL. No. I am delivering the sermon. For you. And then, tomorrow morning, I shall do a rerun for the rest of the congregation so you can show off your very romantic pastor husband.

RUTH. Is this the sermon where I am a joke?

PAUL. You are not a joke, you are referred to as a person who – agh it is funny in context.

RUTH. And this funny romantic sermon, is how long?

PAUL. I don't know, about thirty forty, or fifty minutes?

RUTH. Fifty minutes?!

PAUL. I am telling you Ruth, when God gave me the idea for the sermon I knew in my heart it is a love letter directly to you. By the time I am done you will not remember how long it was, you will be so moved that you will ask me to marry you again or leave me to be a nun for Jesus, one of the two.

RUTH. Every sermon you prepare makes me want to leave you for Jesus Pastor, as you practice on me, every Saturday. But I have this one problem, you see, I do not want your beautiful sermon to be interrupted, and, this person that I met on the street, he is a member of this church and so I invited him to our tea.

PAUL. Oh. Why?

RUTH. Because he is leaving this township tonight and so I said he must come to the church to receive your blessing before he goes.

PAUL. On our anniversary day? Who is this?

RUTH. Remember you do not give up on any member of the church.

PAUL. Who is this.

RUTH. I met Francis.

PAUL. Francis.

RUTH. You do not give up on any / member –

PAUL. No.

RUTH. You / just said so yourself.

PAUL. Francis? Ruth you cannot be serious Francis is no member of this church?

RUTH. He was one of the first people of this township to call you Pastor, how is he not a member of your church?

PAUL. He is leaving? That is a good idea.

RUTH. Good idea? He is being chased out of his own hometown. Thin as a stick, bruises everywhere and he has bandages on his wrists,

PAUL. He has what? Agh the stupidness of this boy.

RUTH. I gave him a hug and he just started crying. For a whole hour he just held my hand and cried. Pastor we must help him. He needs your guidance.

PAUL. I gave my guidance. He rejected it.

RUTH. He does not follow your orders one time and we must all abandon the man?

PAUL. God's orders, not mine –

RUTH. We are His church not His military.

PAUL. Church, military, it does not matter, if we let that boy in here it will break this community. If I say yes to him, I am saying no to everybody else, Ruth. Did you see last month during the whole situation, our attendance was cut in half?

RUTH. If a man has hundred sheep and one of them wanders away, won't he leave the ninety-nine others on the hills and go out to search for the one that is lost?[***]

[***] Excerpt from Matthew 18:12 (NLT).

PAUL. In this township the ninety-nine others are lost too. We have only just begun to find them. I cannot risk the souls of this whole church for one stupid boy.

RUTH. Then nobody else needs to know,

PAUL. It's not / about,

RUTH. Just let us show him God has not forgotten him. Paul please. He said he didn't want to come unless he knew you said yes. I said I will text him.

PAUL. Ruth,

RUTH. I already texted him.

PAUL. Ai yai.

RUTH. This is my anniversary wish. And now I owe you two gifts. Anything you want.

PAUL. My wife is the pastor. I am just the pretty man with the deep loud voice.
Okay.

RUTH. Okay?!

PAUL. I will talk some sense into him and then make you fall in love with me again with my super sermon.

RUTH. I am always falling in love with you again.

PAUL. Ah you just say that because you got your way.

(**RUTH** *gives him an awesome hug.*)

RUTH. Paul. I promise you. To this boy you are the miracle man from God. Thank you.

PAUL. Ha. I had my fair share of miracle people from God. Happy anniversary.

(**CHRIS** *is lingering at the door.*)

RUTH. Oh hello!

CHRIS. Sorry. I'm –

(**CHRIS** *starts to leave.*)

RUTH. No, no please stay.

CHRIS. No I was just,

PAUL. Hello!

CHRIS. Hi.

PAUL. Are you needing assistance?

CHRIS. Excuse me?

PAUL. You are looking like you are lost. What are you looking for?

CHRIS. Do you have to be looking for something to be lost?

PAUL. Generally yes, I think so.

RUTH. I have seen you before, yes?

CHRIS. Oh. I don't –

RUTH. You were here every day this week, at our church.

PAUL. Every day? I did not know! Hello I am the pastor of this church.

CHRIS. I'm not a creepy person, I was just looking. Around.

RUTH. I did not think you were a creepy person. I thought what is this beautiful *mzungu* lady doing here, and I was so very curious but you never came inside so I left you alone.

CHRIS. Thank you.

PAUL. Are you alright?

CHRIS. Hm?

PAUL. You are standing at the door like a child who has done something naughty, would you like to come inside?

CHRIS. Um, yeah. Sure.

(**CHRIS** *takes one step in.*)

RUTH. Welcome to our church.

CHRIS. *Apwoyo matek.*

RUTH. You are very welcome!

PAUL. That is very good!

CHRIS. Ha, thanks. I know two things. Thank you and *Jal – le.*

RUTH. That is very very good!

PAUL. Those two phrases will take you far in this country.

CHRIS. That has been my experience.

RUTH. I am the pastor's wife, Ruth.

PAUL. And I am the pastor's wife's husband, Paul.

CHRIS. Christina. Hi.

PAUL. So what bring you to our township? Are you working with a NGO?

CHRIS. No I'm just visiting for a few days. I grew up here.

RUTH. Are you sure!****

CHRIS. Long ago, as a kid.

PAUL. You were here as a child?

CHRIS. My parents were, missionaries.

RUTH. Are you sure?! It was very difficult time for our country.

CHRIS. I think we left before it got really bad. But this was our church. Built it, brick for brick.

RUTH. What? This was your church? That is fantastic! Pastor this was her church!

PAUL. Yes! Wonderful wonderful.

CHRIS. I wondered if it would still be here, wasn't sure

RUTH. We are all still here. You built a very strong church.

CHRIS. The building, at least.

RUTH. Ha! I must ask you – there is this one, a little picture on the corner.

CHRIS. Little picture?

RUTH. Yes yes it is like a small banana with three circles inside, Please, come come!

> (*They find a little heart engraved into the cornerstone.*)

CHRIS. That's, we did it. Three smiley faces, and our initials at the bottom of each face – me, my mom, my dad. And then I drew a heart around the three. I was eight, so it's a bit, not a heart but.
The first brick we laid.

**** This phrase is used interchangeably with "Really!" in the Ugandan dialect.

RUTH. Ah! I made up so many stories about what this one could be!

CHRIS. My dad had a thing about documenting.

He would've loved to see this.

He should've seen this.

It might've, helped.

RUTH. Our doors are always open whenever he would like to visit.

CHRIS. Oh he can't. He's dead. Last month. He died.

RUTH. Are you alright?

CHRIS. No, I'm [fine].

(RUTH *gives her a very awesome hug.*)

(CHRIS *steps away.*)

Oh, no. Please I don't –

We weren't that close, barely talked for like ten years, strangers, almost, really.

Actually, sorry, I'm just here to, it's a weird – actually, what I need to ask you –

RUTH. Please, how can we help?

CHRIS. I have my dad, his ashes, he left it in his will that we bury him here,

PAUL. Here. Here at our church?

CHRIS. It's weird.

RUTH. Yes it is a little bit strange. That you would bury your dead in our church.

CHRIS. It's not like a coffin, he's in a tree seed. So it would be a seed grave. Not really a grave grave.

He was a weird guy

and he wanted to be a tree at this church.

RUTH. A tree.

CHRIS. This grows into a tree. Mahogany.

RUTH. Haw.

CHRIS. I think he thought, he might finally find some peace, if he came back.

And I thought hey, okay I'll fly eight thousand miles to plant him in a ditch in Africa and maybe we'll have some kind of cozy posthumous father daughter moment closure all that kind of –

I'm just the proxy. You don't have to say yes.

RUTH. Of course we say yes.

PAUL. Ah,

RUTH. It is a tree! I think that will be beautiful in the garden.

PAUL. Ruth we do not have a garden.

RUTH. So the first pastor of this church will be the very first resident of our new garden.

PAUL. I do not know if our African soil will be kind to your tree, but yes it would be an honor.

CHRIS. Oh god, thank you.

RUTH. When do you want a burial? Ceremony?

CHRIS. Oh! No no. We did the funeral, everything, it's fine.

PAUL. So, you want for us to plant the box with your father in it?

CHRIS. Unless you want me to dig the hole, I could dig the hole,

RUTH. Don't worry about that one. You must be so tired. Here, sit down. Would you like some tea?

PAUL. Ruth didn't you say we had another guest soon.

RUTH. Oh he will be a few minutes. We can have some tea and a chat with Christina. She has come such a long way. I will bring more cups. And we should brew more tea.

CHRIS. Actually I'm okay, I just wanted to –

RUTH. We will take care of you, it is no worry. The house is just over there. But of course you know that!

> (**RUTH** *leaves.*)
>
> (*Quiet.*)

CHRIS. Thank you, for the *[gestures: tree seed]*.

PAUL. Of course. How did he pass?

CHRIS. Fatigue. Didn't know people could die of fatigue. He just, got tired of living.

PAUL. He must have loved this church very much.

CHRIS. He did.

What happened to your *[gestures: ear]*.

PAUL. It went missing.

CHRIS. Oh.

PAUL. Every other person in this country has something or other missing from their face.

CHRIS. Of course. I'm sorry. I didn't mean to pry. Sorry.

PAUL. I think I will go help my wife with the tea. Sometimes she forgets to turn the stove off et cetera.

    (**PAUL** *leaves.*)

    (**CHRIS** *is alone.*)

    (*The space. The Skylight. The Space.*)

RUTH. I had no idea today would turn into such a party!

    (**RUTH** *and* **PAUL** *enter.*)

PAUL. Yes, unfortunately we have a guest coming, in a few minutes

RUTH. Pastor what is that.

CHRIS. Oh that's fine, I don't have to stay

RUTH. Stay! Stay! Don't mind our pastor, Chris. He likes to joke. It is only funny in context. Come sit down, both of you, we are floating around like dust clumps. Chris tell me everything, / there are so many rumors of this church.

CHRIS. I don't remember much, rumors?

RUTH. Because of these rumors nobody would come! For the first three months our entire congregation was two people. And I was one of the two people.

PAUL. Ruth,

RUTH. And then Pastor visited every single home in this township. He went door to door, and still these people would not come. What were they saying, Pastor, somebody died in the church, on the day of the / millennium, killed herself or got herself killed.

PAUL. The *Acholi* are superstitious people, they always are saying something happened.

RUTH. Everybody has a different version of the story, ai yai how did your father deal with these people, eh?

CHRIS. I, don't know. He's dead so.

How did you guys end up here?

RUTH. This is the question I ask every day of myself! I am originally from the city but I was seduced by this terrible man. I had this big idea that I would help this country, oh yes, I will march myself to the nearest trauma center, I will educate and help all these broken minds from their war troubles.

PAUL. Let us stop boring our visitor / with the history, and –

RUTH. Of course I very quickly understood I was a stupid girl with more fears then skills. I was so ready to quit and run away until this one came along. After all he has been through, he tries to teach me about Jesus, and get me to go to church with him, sing Jesus songs, but the big trap was this one, Chris, he tells a story to me.

PAUL. Do you want to see more of the church Christina.

RUTH. After I tell my homerun story. When we were getting serious, and I am weighing the good things and bad things about this man – Chris you know the process I am talking about.

CHRIS. Of course.

RUTH. So I am thinking, mmm he is a little bit small, he is a little bit nerd, he is little bit no money and so on,

PAUL. Ruth do we have any ice, I am thirsty for some ice water.

RUTH. Yes, in the kitchen. Anyway so I am on the seesaw a little bit and he knows this so he takes me to a beautiful lake, puts me on a boat like in the American movies yes? And he tells me this story.

PAUL. Ruth, don't –

RUTH. Na uh uh! Girl talk time. If you are embarrassed cover your ears while I show off my romantic pastor huband, eh?

Okay, so once upon a time there is this man, who loved his wife so so much,

and one day the wife really really wanted a piano.

But the man, he was a poor man, so he could not buy a piano. So he collects scraps of cardboard from the market, and he makes a small piano, of the discarded boxes. And then he gives it to his wife. The wife is very very disappointed. So much that she will tear up the piano that he took so very long to make just for her. The wife leaves the house and he thought ah, there she goes, she will find a man who can give her a real piano. But the man cannot forget her. He cannot stop himself from fixing the broken piano. And every day he is playing this piano with his voice, "doon doon doon doon doon doon doon doon," praying for her return.

Finally the wife returns, very guilty. But to her great surprise she finds at the window, the piano, it is fixed. She cries and says I'm sorry, but he says, "My love it is okay. I fixed it."

"Ruth" this man says to me now, "We will break many things but I promise you, I will always always find a way to build it again, if only you can be brave enough to stay." Boom, curtain fall, end of story thank you for playing ladies, Pika belongs to me.

CHRIS. I thought your name was Paul.

RUTH. It is. But I call him Pika, it is his African name.

PAUL. Ruth could you give us a moment alone?

RUTH. Alone?

PAUL. Please.

RUTH. Pastor, stop being so peculiar.

PAUL. Just, please, could you?

RUTH. Chris, my husband is so strange sometimes, we will ignore Pika's –

PAUL. My name is not Pika pleasepleasepleasepl
    will you Leave.

RUTH. …

PAUL. Please.

RUTH. I –

PAUL. Could you.

(**RUTH** *leaves*.)

(*Silence*.)

Start

CHRIS. You look good.

PAUL. Thank you. You too.

(*Silence*.)

CHRIS. I like what you did. With the church. The skylight.

PAUL. Mostly it was Ruth.

CHRIS. She's lovely.

(*Silence*.)

PAUL. Are you, married?

CHRIS. No.

PAUL. It is different in America, the time of marriage I
    think. Here we like to marry our women earlier.

CHRIS. Is that a joke?

(*Silence*.)

PAUL. What do you want. Why are you here?

CHRIS. My dad died. He wanted,

PAUL. That is why you are here? The only reason to come
    all the way –

CHRIS. I don't have to explain anything, to you, of all
    people,

PAUL. If you have returned to revenge –

CHRIS. Revenge?

PAUL. If you have returned so to to ruin / this church –

CHRIS. Why would I want to ruin –

PAUL. – it won't work I have already told them everything.

CHRIS. Wow okay well That's bullshit.

PAUL. I have told them Everything.

CHRIS. Everything?

PAUL. Everything they need to know.

CHRIS. Your wife doesn't know very much.

PAUL. I have experienced many atrocities, they do not
need to hear

CHRIS. About who died? On the millennium, emptying this
church for the past decade and a half?

PAUL. You left. You and your people left and I came back.
You do not know how difficult for me it was to come
back / to face this empty church.

CHRIS. So why? Why? Why did you?

PAUL. I am good for this community. They / see hope,

CHRIS. It's sick! What you, the hole, up there, is it –

PAUL. We needed / more light.

CHRIS. – some kind of shrine? Some kind of –
More Light?

PAUL. It is just a window on a roof.

CHRIS. No it is not.

PAUL. I am trying to fix what is broken, the church, this
township –
You break something, it is okay if you try to fix it, you
said that to me,
we can fix everything, with God's help,

CHRIS. No you can't. No amount of windows on a roof can
fix what you broke.

PAUL. But I will keep trying, we must keep trying, like your
father did for you.

CHRIS. Some guy duck-taped some paper together to shut
his daughter up and then some years later he died, it's
not some grand metaphor to build your new life on,
forgetting the people you've fucked over.

PAUL. Forget? For – Every night, hundred bleeding bodies,
in my dreams / they come together –

CHRIS. Please I don't need your dreams in my –

PAUL. Yours, and Adiel's.

CHRIS. Stop don't say her name please you / don't get to –

PAUL. That is my night every night, Forget? I cannot forget. Do not talk of things you do not know, Chris, / you do not know my troubles, every night

CHRIS. I think I can talk about whatever the fuck I want why are you here at my church?

PAUL. Not your church my church it is my church You left! God's church. It's God's church and God has forgiven me, that is the only way I got better.

Not farms not people, but Grace, The only way how I am now a good man.

CHRIS. Well Good for God but you did not kill God You killed people and they can't forgive you because they are dead and Dead Can't Forgive.

PAUL. I came to this church hoping, at first,

I did not know if she had lived,

CHRIS. She didn't.

(Silence.)

PAUL. Perhaps it was the wrong choice, sick, as you say.

But I had to come back, make it good again,

this is where, somebody was happy about me,

you were happy about me even when you knew how bad I was.

CHRIS. Happy? Were you there? Pika you are the only human on this earth I have aimed and shot / a loaded weapon –

PAUL. You missed. Every shot. A whole round of bullets at point blank and every bullet missed.

CHRIS. Because I was sixteen and didn't know how to shoot a gun.

PAUL. You missed because you did not want to kill me.

CHRIS. I Do want to. Did, want to.

PAUL. You said yes to me.

CHRIS. What?

(PAUL *leaves, maybe to the office.*)

PAUL. You said family, you were happy so happy, you tried to help, remember, you wanted so much for my soul.

CHRIS. What are you / talking about?

(*He returns, tape recorder, from somewhere –*)

I never, what is that. What are you, why do you have that, this is, / that's not yours, it's not yours.

PAUL. You were the first person to say yes to me. You said absolution –

CHRIS. No.

PAUL. – you said yes.

CHRIS. Okay, fine I said yes, and then you killed the one person that –

PAUL. I have killed more than one people, you already knew this. How is it different than what you already said yes to? You are coming here to my church, with your father's ashes, because you are sad, / hurt, struggling –

CHRIS. Back the fuck off about my father.

PAUL. Struggling to bury what is dead, trying to make better what is hurt, we are doing the same thing –

CHRIS. We are not doing the same thing.

PAUL. Yes we are. But you, you are lost in your hurt, you treasure your hurt like it is the castle that makes you special. I am sorry for your suffering but I cannot let my people pay the price for your brokenness. Fight your battles on your own soil and let me fight mine here.

(*Silence.*)

CHRIS. I just want to plant my dead dad and leave, okay? I've wasted my entire adult life trying to leave, this church. I just want to leave.

PAUL. So. Leave.

(*Silence.*)

(FRANCIS *enters.*)

FRANCIS. Excuse me – Hello I am looking for the pastor, do you know where he is?

CHRIS. …

He's –

FRANCIS. Wait I've seen you before?

CHRIS. What?

PAUL. Francis.

FRANCIS. Pastor! This is, oh what is your name, Sarah. Melissa.

PAUL. Now / is not a good –

FRANCIS. Jennifer?

CHRIS. Chris.

FRANCIS. Like the Kardashian?

CHRIS. Um. No. Like short for Christina.

FRANCIS. Christina! Of course! You were very close with my cousin, Adiel.

PAUL. Francis you / must leave us.

CHRIS. Francis –

FRANCIS. You have not changed at all how are you / how is your family!

(**FRANCIS** *gives her an awesome hug.*)

PAUL. Are you deaf boy, I said Go!

FRANCIS. Pastor.

RUTH. Francis, come.

PAUL. Ruth.

RUTH. Let us make ourselves some tea in the house.

FRANCIS. But I thought, Ruth your message, you said –

RUTH. Come, we talk more inside the / house while we wait.

FRANCIS. But you did not invite me? Pastor? You do not want me here?

PAUL. What do you want me to say? You shout out your deeds all around the town, / deliberately go against my advice –

FRANCIS. No Paul I did not tell anyone, / nobody was supposed to know.

PAUL. Nobody was supposed to know? God knows everything.

FRANCIS. I was not talking about God,

PAUL. Why are we not talking about God? Talk about God. Because it is Him you are hurting,

FRANCIS. I am sorry that it is hurting God, hurting so many people that I love,

PAUL. You are not sorry.

FRANCIS. What do you want me to do? I cannot help who I am.

PAUL. Then I cannot help your homo ways heading to hell, but I will not have that in my church.

CHRIS. You can't be serious.

PAUL. Christina, this is not your battle, stay out.

CHRIS. Not my – are you fucking kidding me?

RUTH. Christina, please, I think you must / come back later.

PAUL. Francis and I must get through this together, you have no place –

CHRIS. You're doing to him what you did to me.

PAUL. / That is different.

CHRIS. I think I have a place.

How is it different?

PAUL. I am different. I cannot let my personal guilt blind my judgment in the leadership of this / church, I –

CHRIS. You killed my wife.

> *(Silence.)*

We saved your life and you killed her because I kissed my fucking wife.

RUTH. What?

FRANCIS. Wife? Paul? What / is this one. Ruth?

CHRIS. This is not that different, Pika.

PAUL. / My name is not Pika!

CHRIS. Nothing's changed, you're still a murderer and I am still stuck in that same shithole you've put me in.

PAUL. You put yourself there.

RUTH. Pastor what is she / talking about?

PAUL. All the sins you have committed against the Lord,

CHRIS. My Sins?

PAUL. Your decadence.

CHRIS. What is my sin, Pika. Patching up your face after you put a gun to my head? Letting you run after you shot a bullet into Adiel –

PAUL. I do not cling / to my past with your enthusiasm.

FRANCIS. Adiel?

RUTH. Who is / Adiel?

FRANCIS. No Adiel died here. She shot herself after killing a soldier, Paul and Ruth came only last year.

CHRIS. What do you say every Sunday Pika, to This Community, Thou shalt not lie? Thou shalt not kill? Thou shalt not kill a person, return to the scene of the crime fourteen years later and damn their cousin to hell?

FRANCIS. You were here?

CHRIS. And when you're looking out at these people who trust you and love you and willingly lap up the bullcrap you're feeding them, do you feel Any Guilt? Shame? or has the Grace of God taken care of that too.

RUTH. Pika. What are these people saying?

PAUL. Ruth please, take Francis, away, / Chris and I must –

FRANCIS. You were the soldier.

CHRIS. Chris and I must what? What more / do you want with me?

RUTH. Come Francis we will talk to Pastor after, / I promise, Francis.

FRANCIS. You killed her. We all thought, but it was you? This whole time it was you?

PAUL. I am not perfect, I do not know everything, but every sin is washed clean if –

CHRIS. What if I took a gun and blew out your wife's guts, think we could / clean that up too?

PAUL. Shut up about / my wife! Shut up!

RUTH. Okay Pika / look to me –

CHRIS. If I murdered your wife?

PAUL. That is in the past –

RUTH. It is / alright, I am here, see? Pika look to me.

PAUL. – stop talking about the past.

CHRIS. If it's in the past why are you here.

PAUL. I am trying to fix it!

CHRIS. You are kicking this man out onto the streets, to fix what you did to his cousin?

FRANCIS. How are you a pastor?

RUTH. Francis this is enough

FRANCIS. How is man like you a pastor at my church?

PAUL. I am no longer your pastor, man! I am no longer your – Get out. Get / out get –

RUTH. Paul let us / go, we shall go for a walk, a nice –

PAUL. I am no longer your pastor this is no longer your church.

FRANCIS. And somehow you have the power to tell me, I am going to hell?

PAUL. I do not care where you go get out Get Out –

FRANCIS. I trusted you. I gave you my secret. But you hated me.

RUTH. Francis. Leave.

FRANCIS. You hated me before you even knew me.

RUTH. Get out.

(**FRANCIS** *smashes a window.*)

What are you doing!

PAUL. Francis.

FRANCIS. No.

(**FRANCIS** *picks up a piece of glass.*)

I am not leaving. You want to save my church from my dirty dirty sins this is how you will do it.

(**FRANCIS** *extends the glass toward* **PAUL.**)

PAUL. What are you doing man.

FRANCIS. Do it.

RUTH. Francis stop this stupidness.

(**FRANCIS** *swings his weapon around to* **RUTH.**)

FRANCIS. Shut up stay / there.

PAUL. Ruth stay back!

FRANCIS. You know how to do it, Do it. I'm not the first homo you killed in this church. You can't make me leave my home, everything I know and not pay for it, you can't kick me out turn your eyes and wait for somebody else to bash my head in, I am not going to wait for that, you do it. Do It.

Okay I'll do it. You watch.

(**FRANCIS** *presses the glass to his own throat.*)

RUTH. Francis!

CHRIS. Francis, There are better ways to fight this.

PAUL. This is not what God wants.

FRANCIS. I do not want your God anymore.

PAUL. You know that is not true.

FRANCIS. Do not tell me what I know. You are a liar. You are a joke.

(*He presses.*)

RUTH. Francis Look to me.

FRANCIS. This church is a joke.

RUTH. I was wrong.

I was wrong to ask you to leave.

Pastor is wrong to ask you to leave.

No more. We will do this to you no more.

FRANCIS. No more.

RUTH. I promise you.

We will work this problem out together.

Give that to Pastor.

Please, Francis.

Death is so final.

Right? You know this.

> *(A breath.)*
>
> (**FRANCIS** *gives the bloody glass piece to* **PAUL**.)
>
> (**RUTH** *hits him.*)
>
> *(Wherever she can however she can.)*
>
> *(Slap slap slap.)*

Idiot! Stupid stupid boy, you stupid boy, don't you ever do that again, don't you ever even think about doing something like that again! Ever again / Do you understand? Stupid. Stupid stupid boy, I will kill you if you do that again, understand? Stupid idiot stupid.

CHRIS. Hey hey, it's okay. It's okay, we're good, he's okay we're fine. Calm down, breathe, okay? Come, just take it easy. Everything's alright, it's alright. Shh…

> (**RUTH** *hugs on* **CHRIS** *tightly, a replica of sixteen-year-old* **CHRIS**' *embrace with* **ADIEL** *fourteen years ago.)*

PAUL. Get away from my wife!

CHRIS. …

RUTH. …

PAUL. Get away from my wife Get away from my wife!

> (**PAUL** *bolts toward them and shoves* **CHRIS** *away viciously.)*

Get away from my wife

> *(Shove Shove.)*

I said get away from my wife!

> (**PAUL** *grabs* **CHRIS**, *glass piece still in hand.)*

RUTH. Pika No!

*(***RUTH*** gets in between ***PAUL*** and ***CHRIS***.)*

No.

(He stops.)

(No one moves.)

*(***PAUL*** steps back, glass piece still in hand.)*

PAUL. Everybody knows.

Everybody knows…

RUTH. Paul.

(Like a memory exercise.)

PAUL. Everybody knows, in this story, the traveler is met with some ill fate. First the priest sees the man in pain will he save him No. Second the Levite sees the man in pain will he save him No. Third the Samaritan, somebody that we all hate, somebody we believe is a bad man,

who is the bad man?

Start again. Everybody knows in this story, the soldier is met with some ill fate. First the –

No, not a soldier, a traveler, he is a traveler.

The man the Traveler is beaten, bled, and then left alone by the tree tied to the tree there is no tree –

Haha, Pastor's brain is so sleepy today.

RUTH. Paul look to me.

*(***RUTH*** steps toward him but ***PAUL*** moves away.)*

PAUL. Everybody knows! There is no tree.

First

The Priest, the pastor, I am a pastor now. Everybody knows,

He passes by, sees the man in pain! Will he save him? How can he save him?

He is dead.

He is not dead!

He is lying on the, where is he lying. Why is he lying.

LOVE.

Drains the oxygen, pumps the heart, the blood flows, races through
spills on to her clothes on to this floor on to
no, LOVE. Love, is patient love is kind it does not,
Love is love is –
The blood
of the tree

a gift.
to one who does not deserve.

> (**PAUL** *sees* **CHRIS**.)

Do you hate me now?

> (**PAUL** *places the glass piece in her hands.*)

You said yes You said You said You will fix –
You are a joke. This church is a joke. Everything is still broken and You –

RUTH. Paul. Come. Please.

> (**PAUL** *leaves the church.*)
>
> (*Echo of rain falling into…*)

> (*Very Early Morning.*)
>
> (*The sun is not yet up.*)

(**RUTH** *in the middle of the church.*)

(*Perhaps where we first found* **ADIEL**.)

(*Perhaps she is praying.*)

(*Perhaps she was listening to the tape recorder.*)

(*Either way, that is what she holds in her hand, like a bible or a rosary.*)

(**CHRIS** *comes to the doorway, her carry-on in tow.*)

CHRIS. Hi.

RUTH. Christina.

CHRIS. How are you?

RUTH. …

CHRIS. Is Paul,

RUTH. He has not returned yet.

CHRIS. Oh.

RUTH. He will return.

CHRIS. I'm sorry.

RUTH. What can I do for you?

CHRIS. I just wanted to leave this with –

RUTH. I am very sorry Christina but I do not think we must do that for you. You must bury your dead where it affects You.

CHRIS. Oh, no, that wasn't what – I agree. It would be weird to know your dad is growing into a tree in someone else's backyard.

RUTH. I am sorry we cannot help.

CHRIS. No don't be. He can find peace in my backyard. When I have one. We'll be fine.

That's not why I'm here,

(*A cardboard piano.*)

Couldn't sleep, so I just, I'm not so good with crafts, but.

I'll just leave it here, gotta head out, to catch the bus, Francis is waiting at the,

RUTH. Francis?

CHRIS. Um, yeah. It's, we're on the same bus and, it'd be nice to catch up. So.

    *(***CHRIS*** turns to leave.)*

RUTH. He listened to this one. So much. He listened to it every month sometimes every day.

I never did ask.

It is up to the wife to keep the secrets that our husbands try to keep from us.

A secret flies out to me, and I think I must catch it,

I must be a part of his ribcages and hold them together.

I did not know my silence was suffocating him also.

He is not a bad man, Chris.

He is trying so very hard to be good.

CHRIS. He's lucky to have that. You.

RUTH. I am lucky to have him.

I wish you both safe travels.

CHRIS. Thank you.

Happy Anniversary.

    *(***CHRIS*** leaves.)*

    *(***RUTH*** alone, in church.)*

    *(***RUTH*** turns tape over. Rewind. Hits play.)*

TAPE. This is the wedding of Christina Jennifer Englewood and Adiel Nakalinzi. January 1st, year 2000. I, Chris Blank, take thee, Adiel Nakalinzi, to be my wife, ugh, that's such a dumb word.

To be my wife…

    *(***TAPE*** continues under as the four come together in hymn:)*

JUST AS I AM, WITHOUT ONE PLEA,
BUT THAT THY BLOOD WAS SHED FOR ME,
AND THAT THOU BIDST ME COME TO THEE,
O LAMB OF GOD, I COME, I COME

JUST AS I AM, THOUGH TOSSED ABOUT

WITH MANY A CONFLICT, MANY A DOUBT,
FIGHTINGS AND FEARS WITHIN, WITHOUT,
O LAMB OF GOD, I COME, I COME

JUST AS I AM, OF THAT FREE LOVE
THE BREADTH, LENGTH DEPTH, AND HEIGHT TO PROVE,
HERE FOR A SEASON, THEN ABOVE,
O LAMB OF GOD, I COME,

TAPE. ...With this ring I thee wed, with my body I thee worship, and with all my worldly goods I thee endow: In the name of –

In the name of the Father, and of the Son, and of the Holy Ghost. Amen.

Amen.

End of Play

CPSIA information can be obtained
at www.ICGtesting.com
Printed in the USA
BVOW08s0445060717
488619BV00008B/115/P